This is my book.

My name is

....

Will you please read to me?

Thank you.

THE BEGINNERS BIBLE™

Stories to Sleep On

As told by **Charron E. Taylor**

Illustrated by **Kelly Pulley, Wes Ware,**
and **John Jordan**

RANDOM HOUSE/LITTLE MOORINGS

Library of Congress Cataloging-in-Publication Data
Taylor, Charron E. Stories to Sleep On / by Charron E. Taylor; illustrated by John C. Jordan, Kelly Pulley
and Wes Ware.
p. cm. — (The Beginners Bible)
Summary: A collection of Bible stories containing moral lessons.
ISBN: 0-679-87519-0
1. Bible stories, English. [1. Bible stories.] I. Jordan, John C., 1953- ill.
II. Pulley, Kelly, ill. III. Ware, Wes, ill. IV. Title. V. Series.
BS551.1.T36 1995
220.9´505—dc20 95-33133

First Edition: November 1995

CONTENTS

The day is done, the lights are low.
   You grab a book and to bed you go.

"Please read me a story," you say with a grin.
   I take the book and we both settle in.

I read you stories of heroes from way back when.
   You learn that lessons today are the same as back then.

Your eyes start to flutter as sleep grows near.
   I kiss your cheek and whisper in your ear.

With God each thing is possible no matter how big it seems.
   So take these stories with you into your dreams.

And when you wake, God's love will help you soar
   To places and heights only dreamed of before.

Angel Fireman

Reeeoooow! Reeeoooow!

The sound of a siren filled the air. Six-year-old James and his little sister, Keisha, dashed to the window. James and Keisha clambered up onto the window seat and pressed their noses to the glass, just in time to see a bright red fire engine come barreling down the street.

"I bet my dad's on that fire engine," James cried. James thought his dad was the best firefighter in the world.

"He's not on that truck," Keisha told him. "He's out with Mom someplace."

"Children!" their grandmother's voice rang out from the kitchen. "Come see what I've made!"

James and Keisha scrambled back down off the window seat and ran into the kitchen. Their little noses twitched at the delicious aroma. Sure enough, there on the kitchen counter was a yummy-looking cake.

But why such a special treat? It wasn't James's birthday. And it wasn't Keisha's, either.

"The cake is for your father," their grandmother said. "To celebrate his special award."

"What kind of award?" James asked.

"An award for bravery. He saved Mrs. Lombardi and her daughter from a

fire," explained his grandmother. "They call your father 'The Angel Fireman.'

"The other firefighters are having a ceremony to thank him. That's where your parents are right now. They'll be home any minute, and then we'll have our own party."

"Something sure smells good!" came a voice from the hallway. James and Keisha let out a cheer. "Mom and Dad!"

Their mother carried in the award plaque and set it on the dining room table. Their grandmother set the cake next to the plaque. Soon, the apartment was filled with other firefighters and their families.

Even Mrs. Lombardi and her daughter, Amelia, came to the party. Amelia was Keisha's age. Everyone was laughing and having a good time. James was so proud and happy, he thought he would burst.

"My dad is the best firefighter ever," he announced proudly. "He's 'The Angel Fireman.' "

Mrs. Lombardi smiled and nodded. "That's right, James," she said. "When the fire broke out in our apartment, I prayed to the Lord for an angel to protect us from the flames. A moment later, your father burst through the window. I'm sure that God sent him. That's why I call your dad my 'Angel Fireman.'"

Amelia looked up at James's father with shining eyes and echoed her mother, "Angel Fireman."

"I knew it!" James answered. "My father is the best firefighter in all the world."

James's father looked at his son thoughtfully. "Son," he said. "Come sit by me. I'm a good firefighter, James, and I'm glad you're proud

of me. But I would like to tell you the story of a real angel fireman. Would you like to hear it?"

Now, James had never heard of a real angel fireman, and he was very curious. So he said, "Sure."

A long time ago, a king called Nebuchadnezzar ruled over a land called Babylon. There were lots of different people in Babylon and they spoke many different languages. But there was one way in which they were all the same.

They all had to do exactly what King Nebuchadnezzar told them.

One day, King Nebuchadnezzar called together all of the people who helped him run his government. He made them stand in front of a tall, wide curtain. Then, with a great sound of trumpets, the king's servants pulled back the curtain. When the people saw what was behind it, they were struck speechless and their mouths dropped open in surprise. For behind the curtain was the biggest statue any of them had ever seen!

Then King Nebuchadnezzar said to the people:

"People of many languages, this is my command. As soon as you hear the sound of the horn, the harp, the zither, and the flute, you must fall to your knees and worship this golden statue. If you do not, you will be thrown into a fiery furnace."

Now, none of the people wanted to be thrown into a fiery furnace. That did not sound nice at all! So, as soon as they heard the music, they fell to their knees and worshiped the golden statue. King Nebuchadnezzar was very happy. But he did not stay happy for long.

When the music was over, several people stepped forth to speak. In loud and angry voices, they told King Nebuchadnezzar, "We heard your

command, O King, and we obeyed it. But three men among us who heard it did not obey. They refused to worship your golden statue."

The king frowned and said, "Who are these men who did not obey me?"

And the people answered, "Their names are Shadrach, Meshach, and Abednego."

King Nebuchadnezzar flew into a rage and commanded Shadrach, Meshach, and Abednego to come before him. "I have heard bad things about you," the king said. "But I will give you one last chance.

"If, when you hear the sound of the horn, the harp, the zither, and the flute, you will fall to your knees and worship my golden statue, then I will forgive you. But if you do not, I will have you thrown into the fiery furnace immediately. Not even your god will be able to save you then."

When the other people heard this, they trembled with fear. But Shadrach, Meshach, and Abednego answered:

"We are servants of the most high God and pray to him only. We hear your words, O King, but we are not afraid of your command. Our God can save us from the fiery furnace. But even if he decides not to, we will never worship a golden statue."

When King Nebuchadnezzar heard this, he grew so angry that his face turned purple and his eyes bulged out of his head. "Make my fiery furnace seven times hotter than it has ever been before," he commanded his servants. "Then tie these men up and throw them inside!"

The servants had never seen their king so angry. They jumped to carry out his orders. They made the fire seven times hotter than it had ever been before. Then they tied up the three men and threw them into the fiery furnace.

But no sooner had Shadrach, Meshach, and Abednego hit the flames than King Nebuchadnezzar cried out in amazement, "What is going on here?

I thought you threw three men into the flames."

"We did, O King," the servants answered.

"Then how," asked King Nebuchadnezzar, "can you explain this? I see four men walking around in the fiery furnace. The fire hasn't hurt them at all. And one of them looks like an angel, keeping the others safe from the flames."

When none of his servants could explain this, King Nebuchadnezzar approached the mouth of the fiery furnace and called out:

"Shadrach, Meshach, and Abednego, servants of the most high God, come out of the fiery furnace. Come here to me!"

So Shadrach, Meshach, and Abednego stepped out of the fiery furnace, and all of the people crowded around. Now, Shadrach, Meshach, and Abednego were a sight to see. For the fire had not touched them. Not so much as a hair on their heads was singed. Then King Nebuchadnezzar said to his people:

"Praise be to the God of Shadrach,

Meshach, and Abednego. For, when they trusted him, and would worship no other, he sent his angel to save them from the flames. No other god can save in this way."

And King Nebuchadnezzar let Shadrach, Meshach, and Abednego go home. From that day on, no one had to bow down to the statue ever again.

"So," said James, when the story was over, "Shadrach, Meshach, and Abednego put their trust in God and they weren't afraid of the raging fire."

Mrs. Lombardi said, "And when our apartment was on fire, I prayed to God, and he sent your father, my own angel fireman, to protect us from the raging fire."

James had to admit he was impressed with the first angel fireman. "You're still my hero, Dad," he said. "But I guess you're the second greatest firefighter in all the world."

James's father gave James a big bear hug. "That's good enough for me, son," he said.

"Now, would anyone like to guess what kind of cake this is?" asked James's grandmother.

"I would. It's angel food cake!" James said. And everybody laughed.

Then James, his father, and all the guests had a slice of Grandma's delicious angel food cake.

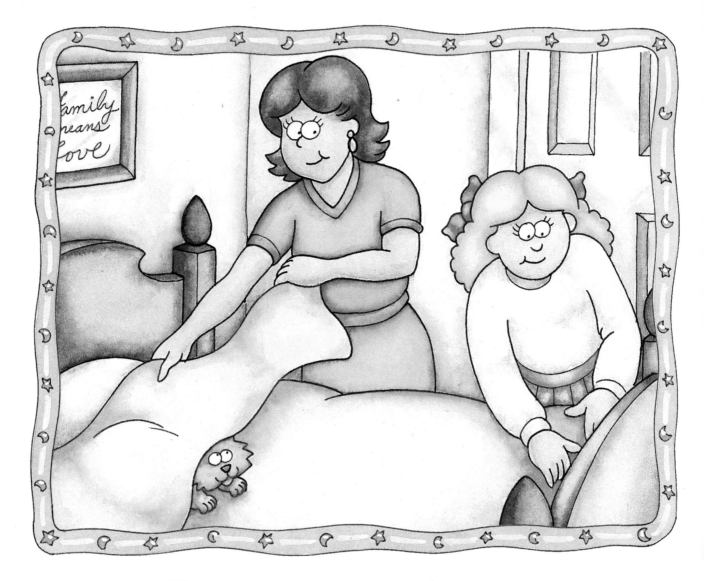

Lesson in Love

"Why is Grandma coming to live here?" Molly asked as she watched her mother carry sheets into the spare bedroom. "I thought she had a house of her own."

"She did," answered her mother. "But she sold it after Grandpa died. The new owners are just now moving in, so your grandma needed

somewhere to go."

"Molly," said her mother. "Please help me make the bed." Molly took the end of the sheet and tucked it under the mattress.

Molly and her mother had lived by themselves for as long as she could remember. "But why is she moving in here?" Molly asked. "It's so far away from where she lives now."

"I asked your grandmother to move in with us, Molly. I wanted her to be with her family. I didn't want her to be all alone. When your father died, I was very sad. I felt all alone. I asked God to help me. And guess whom he sent?"

"Who?" asked Molly.

"Your grandmother," her mother answered. "She was a great comfort to me. You were just a baby, and she loved us both so much. It was a difficult time for me. But because of her love and support, we pulled through."

"Catch!" said her mother. And she tossed Molly a pillowcase.

Molly thought about her grandmother while she wrestled with the pillowcase. She remembered the time when her mom was sick and Grandma had come to take care of her. She had helped Molly learn her ABCs. And she had taught her how to grow seedlings on her windowsill.

"Thank you, Molly," her mother said when they were finished. Together, they looked around the room. "I think this room needs some color," her mother said.

"I know what we can do," said Molly. "Let's pick some flowers from the garden. Grandma loves flowers." So Molly and her mother went out into the garden to pick some flowers for Grandma's new room.

Molly loved the garden. The flowers smelled good and they always made her feel happy. But the thing she liked best was that she and her mom had planted the garden together.

"Do you remember what a good time we had planting this garden?" Molly's mother asked as she and Molly picked some sweet peas.

Molly sniffed a sweet pea. "Yes, I do."

"Guess who taught me how to care for a garden?" Molly's

mother asked.

"Grandma?" Molly guessed.

"Yes!" said her mother. "Isn't it amazing how beautiful the flowers are now? Remember when we planted the tiny seeds and, as we took care of them, they grew into a beautiful flower garden? That's why I want Grandma to come and live here."

"So we can plant a garden?" asked Molly.

"No, silly," said her mother. She ruffled the top of Molly's hair. "So we can do things together. We can love each other and take care of each other, the way that families do."

"Oh," said Molly. She thought she was beginning to understand.

"We'll be like Ruth and Naomi in the Bible," said her mother. Molly was curious.

"Who are Ruth and Naomi?"

"Let's go find a vase for these flowers," her mother answered. "And I'll tell you."

A long time ago, there was a young woman named Ruth. She lived with Naomi, her mother-in-law, in a place called Moab.

Then a sad thing happened.

Naomi's husband died. Soon after, Ruth's husband died, too.

Naomi was unhappy, and she felt very lonely. She was far away from where she'd grown up. So she said to Ruth, "It is time for you to go back to your own family. It won't do you any good to stay with me. For I have decided to move back to Bethlehem, the place where I grew up. I want to be near my family."

But Ruth loved Naomi. She knew she would miss her if she moved away. So she said, "I will come with you."

Naomi didn't think this was a good idea. "You are young," she told Ruth.

"You might want to get married again. You should stay here with your family and friends. You will be happier here."

But Ruth said to Naomi, "Please stop asking me to stay here without you, for that is something I will not do. Where you go, I will go. Where you stay, I will stay. Your family will be my family and your God, my God."

Naomi knew that Ruth was serious about coming to Bethlehem with her. The two of them set out together to make the long journey to Naomi's old home.

When they got to Bethlehem, Naomi's family was surprised to see her. She had been gone for a long time.

Ruth and Naomi found a small house where they could live. Times were hard, and they were very poor. They asked God to take care of them. Then Ruth decided she could help by going out and picking up the grain left behind by workers in the fields around the city of Bethlehem.

All day long, Ruth worked in the hot sun gathering leftover grain. Then, each night, she brought a little grain home to Naomi so that they would have something to eat. Ruth

was tired when she got home. Naomi worked hard, too. They were glad to be in their new home.

One day, the man who owned one of the fields noticed how hard Ruth was working.

"Who is that young woman?" he asked.

"Ruth," replied the other workers. "She left her own home and traveled all the way to Bethlehem so that she could take care of Naomi, her mother-in-law."

Now the man, whose name was Boaz, had heard of Ruth. Boaz liked the way that Ruth was taking care of Naomi.

"Make sure to leave extra grain for Ruth to pick up," he told his workers. "For she is doing a kind and loving thing." The workers did as Boaz asked, and Ruth and Naomi were very thankful, because they always had plenty to eat.

When Ruth found out that Boaz had helped her, she went to thank him. But Boaz told Ruth that she was the one who should be thanked. The more Boaz got to know Ruth, the more he liked her. And the more Ruth got to know Boaz, the more she liked him. So one day, Boaz asked Ruth to marry him. This made both Ruth and Naomi very happy.

"So Ruth and Naomi loved each other and took care of each other. They were a family and that's what families do," said Molly.

"That's right, Molly," said her mother.

"Now do you know why I asked Grandma to come and live with us?"

"Yes, I do," said Molly. "And you know what? I want Grandma to come live here, too."

15

Just at that moment, there was a knock at the door. Molly dashed to answer it. When she opened the door, her grandmother was standing there, holding the most beautiful roses she had ever seen.

"Grandma, I'm so glad you've come to live with us!" she exclaimed, throwing her arms around her grandmother.

"Look, Grandma, we picked these flowers for your room," said Molly as she held out the vase of flowers.

Molly's grandmother smiled and said, "And I brought these roses from my garden for you."

"I know exactly where we should plant them," Molly said.

She took her grandmother's hand and led her out to the patio. With a heartwarming smile, Molly said, "If we give them lots of love and take care

of them, they will grow into a beautiful rose garden, just like our family has grown."

Where's My Lunch?

Brrring. Brrring.

The sound of the lunch bell was loud in the classroom. Todd put away his spelling book and raced to get his lunch. He was very hungry. He was glad it was lunchtime.

But Todd was in for a big surprise! He couldn't find his lunch anywhere. Had somebody stolen his lunch?

Todd didn't know what to do. Was somebody being mean? Todd didn't think he'd made anyone mad enough to take his lunch, but he couldn't think of any other reason why his lunch would be missing.

"Aren't you hungry, Todd?" asked his teacher, Miss Mills. She had come to stand next to him while he was

deciding what to do.

Todd liked his teacher. He thought she was the prettiest teacher in the whole school. If he told her about his lunch, he decided, she would know just what to do.

"My lunch bag is missing," he said, looking down at his tennis shoes. "I guess somebody doesn't like me. Did I do something wrong?"

"Of course not," Miss Mills said immediately. "And you have lots of friends. I have an extra big lunch today, Todd, and it's a nice sunny day. Why don't we sit outside and you can share my lunch with me."

So Todd sat with Miss Mills and they shared lunch together.

"I knew I could tell

you about my missing lunch, Miss Mills," Todd said when lunch was almost over. "I knew you were a nice teacher, but I didn't think you would share your lunch with me!"

"You know, this reminds me of a story I know. It is about Elijah," said Miss Mills as they shared the last chocolate chip cookie. "He was a great man and he didn't have any food, either. But someone took care of him."

"Who?" Todd wanted to know.

"His teacher?"

"Yes," Miss Mills answered. "But Elijah's teacher was God."

Elijah lived in a time when many people had forgotten God. They didn't remember his commands. They didn't live the way God wanted them to. They did mean things. This made God very unhappy. So God told Elijah to go talk to the king.

"Because you have forgotten God," Elijah told the king, "there will be no rain for a very long time."

For days and days, no rain fell from the sky. The crops could not grow, because there was no rain to water them. Soon, people were running out of food. Even Elijah was running out of food. Elijah prayed. So God took care of Elijah and told him what to do.

God showed Elijah a brook with fresh running water. He told Elijah he would send ravens to bring him food every morning and every night. And he told Elijah to drink the fresh water from the brook.

Elijah did everything just as God told him to.

More days passed, and more days, and still no rain fell from the sky. Soon

Elijah's brook dried up. He wondered what he would do for food now. Elijah prayed again. Once again, God took care of him and told him what to do.

"Go to a nearby town," God told Elijah. "There is a woman who lives there who will give you food."

So Elijah went to the town. When

he got to the town gates, he saw a woman gathering wood.

"Will you please bring me a drink of water?" Elijah asked. "And may I have a piece of bread?"

But the woman was worried that she couldn't help Elijah. "I don't have any bread," she replied. "I only have a little bit of flour and a little bit of oil. I am gathering wood so that I can go home to my son and bake one last loaf of bread for us. After that, our food will be gone."

"Don't be afraid," Elijah told the woman. "Go home and do just as you planned, only make some bread for me, too. God has told me that your flour and oil will not run out before it rains again. There will be enough for all of us, you'll see."

So the woman went home and baked the bread and gave some to

Elijah. And when they had finished eating, she looked at her supplies. Sure enough, there was still some flour and oil left over, just as Elijah had said there would be.

God took good care of them. And the woman, her son, and Elijah had food to eat every day.

"Elijah was a lot like me, wasn't he?" Todd asked his teacher. "He didn't do anything wrong, but he still didn't have any food. In fact, he did everything right, and he made new friends, too."

Todd smiled at his teacher. "Thank you for sharing your lunch with me." All of a sudden, there was a loud rustling in the bushes next to the bench. A moment later, a squirrel

24

appeared. He was chewing on a peanut butter and jelly sandwich.

"Hey," Todd cried. "That's my sandwich! Do you suppose the peanut butter sticks to the roof of his mouth? It sure gets stuck to mine!"

Miss Mills started laughing. Todd laughed, too. At the sound of their laughter, the squirrel dropped the sandwich and scurried away. Todd was glad he'd had lunch with Miss Mills. She had helped him remember

that God would take care of him, just like he took care of Elijah.

"I'm sure glad that you're my teacher," Todd said.

Then the school bell rang and they both headed back to class.

The Watchman

"Mom?" Stephanie said as she looked around the mall. She couldn't see her parents anywhere. "Dad? Mom?"

The mall was full of people. There were lots of different things to see. Stephanie had been having a good time shopping for a birthday present for her little brother, Jason. But now she couldn't find her parents and she didn't know what to do.

Stephanie was all by herself, with no friends to help her. All of a sudden, she felt very lost and very scared. That was when she remembered something her mother always said.

"Whenever you feel lost or lonely, Stephanie, you can ask God to help you. He always knows just what to do, and he's always watching over you."

So Stephanie decided that this was a good time to ask for God's help. "Please, God," she whispered. She tried hard not to cry. "I'm lost and afraid, and I don't know what to do. Will you please send someone to help me find my mom and dad?"

"Are you okay?" said a friendly voice above her. Stephanie raised her head. Standing next to her was a man in a blue uniform. He had on a big black name tag and a shiny gold badge.

"My name is Sam," he said, pointing to his name tag. "I'm in charge of mall security."

"What's mall security?" Stephanie asked.

"It means I watch over things," Sam answered. "And you look like you could use some help."

"I do need help," Stephanie answered. "I can't find my mom and dad."

"Don't you worry," Sam told her. "I know just what to do. This little girl has lost her parents," he said to the lady behind the cash register. "I'm going to take her to my office and get some help. If her parents come back here, will you tell them where we went?"

"Will do," said the lady. So Stephanie went with Sam.

"What's your name?" Sam asked her as they walked through the mall.

"My name is Stephanie," she answered. "I'm shopping for a birthday present for my little brother, Jason."

Sam's office was in the middle of the mall. It had big windows and Stephanie could see all the people shopping. She watched them while Sam made a phone call.

"Who did you call?" she asked when he was finished.

"I called my helpers," Sam said. "There are more than twenty of them. Don't worry. They'll help find your mom and dad."

"I'm not worried anymore," Stephanie told him. "I asked God to send someone to help me and you came along."

Sam's face lit up with a big grin. "Do you know something, Stephanie?" he said. "When I get scared, that's just what I do!

"It helps me to know that God is always watching over me. And I know a great story about somebody else who asked for God's help when he was scared. Would you like to hear it while we wait for your mom and dad?"

"Sure," Stephanie answered.

"This story is about Daniel," Sam said.

Daniel worked for a king named Darius. King Darius had an enormous kingdom. It was so big, the king was worried. "My people need me," King Darius thought. "But how can I know what they need when my kingdom is so big?"

So King Darius decided to appoint 120 governors to help him run his kingdom. That way the governors could tell him what the people might need. King Darius liked his plan. He appointed his 120 governors right away.

But having 120 governors didn't help King Darius at all! The king never got a moment's peace. Every

minute of every day, one of his 120 governors wanted to ask him something. So King Darius made a second plan. He appointed three presidents to answer the questions of the governors. Daniel was one of these three men.

The king liked Daniel very much. He saw that Daniel did good work, and that he was wise and trustworthy. Daniel always answered the governors' questions, no matter what time it was.

And King Darius saw that Daniel prayed to his God three times each day. The king knew that Daniel's God was very powerful. And he knew that Daniel would always serve his God.

One day, King Darius decided that he was so proud of Daniel that he wanted to give him a big promotion. He'd put Daniel in charge of the other two presidents and all the governors in his kingdom. Only the king would be more important.

When the presidents and governors heard what the king was planning to do, they were

not happy at all! They didn't like Daniel. In fact, they were jealous of him. The presidents and governors didn't want King Darius to be proud of Daniel. They wanted the king to be proud of them. So they tried to think of something that would make Daniel look bad.

"We can never make him look bad because of his work," they decided. "He's too good at what he does. But maybe we can get him into trouble

because of the way he's always praying to his God." They thought and they thought, and at last they came up with a plan. Then they went to see King Darius.

"King Darius, may you live forever," the presidents told him. "We have written a new law, and we'd be honored if you'd sign it. For the next thirty days, no one in your kingdom can pray to any other man or god. They can only ask things of you.

Anyone who disobeys this law must be thrown into the lions' den."

Now, King Darius liked the new law. He liked the idea that only he could grant his people what they asked for. So he agreed with his presidents and signed the law. Then he sent his messengers to proclaim it throughout his kingdom.

The presidents were happy that their plan was working. They went to Daniel's house to see what he would do.

When Daniel heard about the king's new law, he knew he was in trouble. According to this law, he could pray only to King Darius. He could not pray to God. What should he do? For a moment, Daniel thought that perhaps he should stop praying to God. After all, the law was only for thirty days. But then he realized that wasn't a good thing to do.

"I cannot turn away from God," Daniel said to himself. "If I serve God faithfully and put my trust in him, I'm sure that he will take care of me."

When it came time for evening prayers, Daniel knelt down and said his prayers as usual. He asked for God's help. The presidents and governors saw everything that Daniel did. They ran quickly to tell the king.

"King Darius!" they cried. "Someone has broken your law!"

"Who has dared to do such a thing?" the king shouted.

"Daniel has," they cried triumphantly. "You must throw him to the lions at once."

When the king heard this, he was very unhappy. He saw that the governors and presidents had tricked him into making a law that Daniel could not obey. The king tried to think of a way to save Daniel. But he could not. He had to send for Daniel. He had to tell him that he had broken the law.

"Daniel, you have broken my law. You must be thrown into the lions' den. I hope your powerful God will watch over you and save you from the lions," King Darius told him. Then the

king had Daniel thrown into the lions' den. A huge stone was rolled in front of the opening so that there was no way for Daniel to get out. With a heavy heart, King Darius went home.

All night the king wondered if Daniel was all right. As soon as the first rays of sun peeped over the horizon, King Darius leapt out of bed and hurried to the lions' den.

"Daniel," he called, "are you still alive? Has your God, whom you serve so faithfully, watched over you? Has he saved you from the lions?"

"Yes, he has, King Darius," Daniel called out. "I am still alive. My God was with me in the lions' den. He sent his angel to shut the mouths of the lions."

Daniel came out of the lions' den without a single scratch. King Darius was overjoyed.

"Let us praise Daniel's God," King Darius said to his people. "He listened to the prayers of his faithful servant and saved him from the lions."

And all of the people praised Daniel's God.

"That's a great story," Stephanie exclaimed when Sam was finished. "I was just like Daniel, wasn't I? I asked God for help when I was in trouble, and he sent you."

"Stephanie! There you are!" her

parents cried as they came through the doorway. Stephanie ran over to her mom and dad.

"We were so worried," her mother told her. "Are you all right?"

"Fine," Stephanie answered. "When I got scared, I remembered what you told me. I asked for help from God, and he sent Sam to take care of me."

"That's my girl," said Stephanie's father. He reached out to shake Sam's hand. "Thank you for watching over our daughter," he told him.

"My pleasure," Sam said. Stephanie and her family told Sam good-bye.

"Well, Stephanie," said her mother. "Do you know what you want to get Jason for his birthday?"

"I do, Mom," Stephanie answered. "But I want it to be a surprise."

The next day was Jason's birthday. Stephanie could hardly wait for him to open his present from her. Jason pulled the wrapping paper off the box and opened the lid. He squealed in delight when he saw what was inside.

"It's a lion!" Jason shouted.

"Now I want to tell Jason the story of Daniel," Stephanie said. "That way, he'll know that God watches over us. He will take care of us when we're lost and alone. And we don't have to be afraid."

"Right, Mom and Dad?" said Stephanie.

"That's right, Stephanie!" her parents said.

The Wise Man

It was a Saturday, and Lynn and her mom were spending the afternoon at the park just down the street from her home. It was her favorite way to spend the afternoon, particularly when the gardener was working. The gardener was very old, and he was very patient. He always answered every question that Lynn asked.

"What are you doing?" asked Lynn as she walked over and stood next to the gardener.

"I'm decorating the park with these flowers for this summer's garden show," he said as he unloaded flowers from his truck. Then he carefully lined them up in front of a flower bed and began digging holes.

"Why are you planting those flowers so far apart?" Lynn asked the gardener.

"I plant them far apart to give them room to grow," he told her. He set a plant with a bright red flower into a hole. Carefully, he patted the soil around it to make sure the plant was snug and secure. Then he scooted over a little, made another hole, and did it again.

"Oh," said Lynn. "That makes sense. What are they called?"

"These are geraniums," the gardener told her. "They're my favorites because they're so big and red. I have just a few more to plant."

"Then what will you do?" Lynn asked.

"I'll plant some yellow marigolds in

front of the red geraniums," the gardener answered.

"Why?"

"I think yellow and red are pretty together. And marigolds help keep insects away."

"What color comes after yellow?"

"Pink," said the gardener.

"When I'm finished with the marigolds, I'm

going to plant those pink flowers, called impatiens, underneath that big oak tree."

Lynn was curious. "Why don't you just put them next to these?"

"Because impatiens' favorite place to grow is in the shade," the gardener answered. "And there's lots of shade under that old oak tree."

Lynn was very impressed. The gardener knew which flowers kept insects away, and he knew where different kinds of flowers liked to grow.

"How do you know all of this?"

The gardener leaned back on his heels and laughed.

"Well, I started out by asking lots of questions, just like you."

"Do you know what I think?" Lynn asked the gardener as she followed him over to the old oak tree. "I think you're the wisest man in the world."

But the gardener shook his head. "Come help me plant these impatiens," he invited Lynn, "and I'll tell you the story of Solomon. He was a truly wise man."

Solomon was a king who lived a very long time ago. He was a young king, and he wanted to rule over his people wisely. Solomon always thought long and hard about what was best for his people. But no matter how long and hard he thought, sometimes Solomon didn't know what to do.

One night, God came to visit Solomon in a dream. "Ask me for something, Solomon," God said, "and I will give it to you."

"Lord," Solomon answered, "how can I rule wisely? How can I be a better king? I am trying very hard, but I don't always have the answers. So, if you want to give me a gift, I ask you for wisdom. Then I will be a better king."

God was pleased with what Solomon had asked for.

"I will grant your request, Solomon," God told him. "I will give you a wise heart. No one will ever be as wise as you are. And because you put your people first and did not think only of yourself, I will give you great wealth and honor. If you continue to be a good king, I will also give you a long life."

Solomon had asked the right questions, and God blessed him. Solomon was overjoyed with God's gifts. And he said many prayers and prepared a great feast to give thanks to God.

Solomon continued to be a good king to his people. He made his decisions carefully. And because Solomon listened and learned, his people grew and became strong. People came from other nations and said that Solomon's city was the most beautiful in all the world.

One day, Solomon felt sad that he hadn't built a place for God. So he selected a hilltop with a magnificent

view. On it he built a beautiful temple so that all of his people would have a place to worship God.

It took Solomon's workers seven years to build the temple. When everything was finished, Solomon called his people together. Then he knelt down and said a special prayer to God.

"There is no God like you," Solomon said. "Not in heaven and not on earth. You keep your promises to those who obey you. You give us your strength to make us wise and strong."

Solomon and his people had a great festival to celebrate their love for God. The people were glad that Solomon had built the temple for them

to pray in. They were glad that God had given them such a wise king.

"You were right," Lynn said as she and the gardener finished planting the impatiens. "Solomon was a very wise man."

"That's right," said the gardener. "He cared for all the people, and his kingdom grew and grew until it was the most beautiful kingdom ever known."

Lynn was quiet for a moment as she helped the gardener dig a hole.

"I'd like to ask you just one more question," she said when she was finished.

"What?" asked the gardener.

"May I help you work in the garden? That way I can learn more, and maybe one day I'll be wise like you and Solomon."

The gardener liked Lynn's last question. He didn't have any trouble answering it at all.

"Yes, I'll let you work in my garden, and I'll tell you what," said the gardener. "Because you've asked so many fine questions and want to learn, I'm going to give you your very own flower bed."

"Really?" asked

Lynn in an excited voice.

"Yes," said the gardener. "You can choose whatever flowers you want. And after you've planted your flowers, and taken special care of them, we'll watch them grow into a beautiful garden. In fact, you can enter a flower in the contest they have every year at the garden show."

"Will my friends get to come and see them?" asked Lynn.

"Why, sure they can. Almost everyone in town comes to see the garden show," answered the gardener.

"Really? Can I enter the pink impatiens?"

"Yes. But you better get started right away."

"You know what?" Lynn said. "This is going to be the best summer ever. I get to have my own flower garden, and even enter a contest. I can't wait!"

Moving Day

Vroom. Vroom.

The moving van came roaring down the street. Sitting on the front steps of his new house, Jesse looked the other way. Jesse didn't want to live in Texas. He wanted to live in Arizona, where he'd been born. His dad had been given a new job, and so the family had to move.

Jesse missed Arizona. He missed his old house and he missed his school. But most of all, he missed his friends.

The moving van rumbled to a stop in front of Jesse's new house. The movers jumped out and got right to work. Jesse rested his chin in the palms of his hands and stared at the movers stubbornly. They'd have to go right by him to get into the house, and Jesse wasn't about to get out of the way. He didn't want to make things easy for the movers. He didn't want this new place to be his home.

"Maybe you'd better scoot over," one of the movers told him as they carried the couch up the front walk. "I don't want you to get hurt."

Jesse glared at him. He didn't want to scoot over. He wanted to be in the way.

"Son," his father's voice called from inside the house. "Move over now. Stay out of the way."

Jesse knew he needed to do what his dad told him. So he got up off of the steps. He watched the movers going back and forth. And he was very unhappy.

"Okay, guys, it's twelve o'clock. Let's break for lunch," said one of the movers.

The sun was hot in the sky when the movers sat down to eat their lunch. Jesse's mother brought out some ice-cold lemonade. Everyone was having a good time. Everyone, that is, but Jesse.

When lunch was over, the concerned mover came over to talk to Jesse. "You look a little down in the dumps," he said. "Is anything wrong?"

"I don't want to be here," Jesse burst out, unable to contain himself another minute. "I want to go back to Arizona."

The mover nodded his head sympathetically. "I've moved lots of people in my day, and I know moving can be hard. But your folks seem to

just what they're doing."

Jesse scuffed the dirt a little with his shoe.

"I know a story about a man who had to move without knowing anything about where he was going," the mover continued. "Would you like to hear his story? He had the same name as I do."

"What's your name?" Jesse asked.

"Abe," the mover answered. "It's short for Abraham."

Well, Abraham lived in the same place all his life. Until one day, God told Abraham that he wanted him to move.

"I want you to leave the place where you grew up and go to a new place I will show you," God told him.

Now, Abraham liked where he was living. He liked the place where he'd grown up. But Abraham knew he should listen to God. So he packed his bags and prepared to do as God had asked.

Then God told Abraham that he didn't have to go to his new home alone. His family could come along, too. So Abraham's wife, Sarah, helped him get ready for their long journey.

Abraham's nephew Lot helped, too. God hadn't asked Lot to go on the trip, but Lot wanted to go anyway.

They packed all of their belongings—their tents, dishes, clothing, and food. Then they gathered together their animals and the people who helped take care of the herds. At last, they were ready. Abraham and his family set out on their journey, just as God had told them to do.

They traveled for a long time, and finally they came to a beautiful green valley. It was a wonderful place, but

Abraham was afraid that there wasn't enough room for all of them. He wondered what he should do.

Then Abraham's helpers and Lot's helpers started quarreling. They argued and they argued and they would not stop. So Abraham said to Lot, "It's not a good idea for all of us to live together. There are too many of us and there isn't enough room." Lot agreed with Abraham.

Then Abraham said, "I will let you have the first choice of where to live. If you go to the right, then I'll go to the left. And if you go to the left, then I'll go right. That way, we won't be too close together." So Lot looked around to see where he wanted to live.

Lot saw that the valley in front of him was green and beautiful. There was plenty of water and lots of land for his animals. The valley was the nicest place for miles around. So Lot chose the green valley for himself. He told his uncle, "I will live here." And Abraham continued on his journey.

Finally, Abraham and Sarah found a place to live. It was near a grove of trees in a place called Hebron. When Abraham had pitched his tents, God came to visit him.

"Lift up your eyes," God said to

Abraham, "and look all around you. Be sure to look in every direction. All the land that you can see, I give to you and your children, forever."

Abraham could hardly believe it. He was overjoyed to have such a gift from God. But God wasn't finished yet.

"I will give you many children, Abraham," God told him. "You will have so many children, grandchildren, and great-grandchildren that they will be like the grains of dust in a dust storm. Nobody will be able to count them. You will be very happy. Now go and walk through this new land."

Abraham did as God had asked him. As he walked, he was filled with excitement about his new home. So Abraham thanked God for everything that he had given him.

"I like that story," Jesse said when the mover had finished. "So Abraham had to leave his home and friends. But he trusted God. And God had known just what he was doing when he told Abraham to move."

"That's right," said Abe. "And I'll bet if you looked around, you'd find

your new neighborhood is pretty nice, too."

Jesse looked around with new interest. "Hey," he said. "There's a boy in the yard next door. He's looking right at me!"

"Why don't you go over and introduce yourself?" suggested Abe. And that's just what Jesse did.

The movers continued unloading the truck while Jesse got to know his new neighbor. When the movers were all finished, Jesse went to tell Abe good-bye.

"Abe, this is Martin," Jesse told

him. "He's got a trampoline and he lives right next door."

"That's great," Abe answered. "I'm sure you guys will be good friends. Good-bye now." Jesse waved as the moving truck roared away.

"Jesse?" called his father. "Can you help me move some of these things into your room?"

"Sure, Dad," Jesse answered. "I'll see you later," he told Martin. "Right now, I have to help my dad."

"Okay," said Martin. "Maybe when you're all done, you can come back over and play."

"That'd be great," Jesse answered. "And maybe I can show you my room."

"This is a nice house, Dad," Jesse told his father as the two of them set up his bed. "I think I'm going to like living here after all."

Friends

"Oh, Mom," cried Valerie as she put her head down in her hands.

Valerie's mother sat down next to her, "What's the matter, sweetheart?" she asked.

"I don't feel too good about myself," said Valerie.

"Why do you say that?" Valerie's mom asked.

"There's a new girl at school, Mom," she said. "She's really smart, but everyone was making fun of her. Today, one of the other girls taped a sign that said 'teacher's pet' on her back and she didn't even feel it. She walked around with the sign on her back for the whole day."

Valerie's mother took a sip of milk

before she said anything. "You saw the sign and didn't do anything about it?" she asked.

Valerie shook her head no and asked what she should have done.

"I want to tell you a story, Valerie," said her mother.

"Who's the story about?" Valerie asked.

"The story is about a young lady named Esther," her mother answered.

Esther lived in the land of Persia. Xerxes was the name of Persia's king. One day, King Xerxes decided that he wanted a queen. So he looked throughout his kingdom for a beautiful young maiden. Esther turned out to be the most beautiful one of all. So Xerxes made Esther his queen and she went to live with him in the palace. Everyone was very happy for a while.

King Xerxes had many people to

help him rule his kingdom. A man named Haman was one of them. Haman was proud and selfish, though King Xerxes didn't realize this.

Haman thought he was better than other people. He wanted everyone to bow down to him.

There was one man who refused to bow down. His name was Mordecai. He was Queen Esther's cousin. But Haman didn't know that.

When Haman learned that Mordecai would not bow down to

him, he got very angry. He had hurt Haman's pride in front of everybody. This could not be allowed to go on!

So Haman made a plan to get rid of Mordecai and his people, the Jews. Then he went to see King Xerxes.

"I have just heard some terrible news," Haman told the king. "But I know just what to do about it."

Haman's words alarmed King Xerxes. "What is this news?" he asked.

"There are people living in your kingdom who do not respect your

do. He had to go and see his cousin, Queen Esther.

Mordecai urged Esther to go to the king and try to save her people. He urged Esther to ask the king to change his law. But when Esther heard Mordecai's words, she trembled.

"There are very strict rules in the palace," Esther told her cousin. "And one of the rules says that no one may talk to the king unless he asks you to. If I even show up in his throne room when I haven't been invited, he can put me to death."

Now Mordecai understood why Esther was afraid. But still, he urged her to speak to the king. Only she

rulers. They do not respect me," Haman told him. "It's dangerous to let them stay here. They don't do things the way we do."

"You're right, that is terrible news," agreed the king. "What do you think I should do?"

"I think you should destroy them," Haman answered. "If you do, I'll give you lots of money."

King Xerxes wrote the command as Haman requested. It said that all of Mordecai's people were to be destroyed. Haman was very happy. He would soon do away with Mordecai and all of his people.

When Mordecai heard about the king's command, he got very upset. He knew that there was only one thing to

could stop Haman and the new command. Esther was still very frightened. But she knew she had to do what was right, in spite of her fears. She was the only one who could save her people. Esther knew she had to go and speak to the king.

The king was glad to see Queen Esther. She invited the king and Haman to a party. The king went. When Haman showed up, Queen Esther approached the king and said, "If I have made you happy, King Xerxes, please grant my request. Do not destroy my people, as you have commanded. Let them live in peace."

Now the king was stunned to hear that Queen Esther's people were to be destroyed. "Who requested that I command this terrible thing?" he asked.

"Haman did," answered Queen Esther, pointing to where Haman stood. "He wants you to destroy me and my people."

Now King Xerxes saw that Haman had tricked him, and this made the king very mad. "Tell your people to protect themselves until I can write another command," the king told Esther. Then he had Haman taken away.

Esther was happy that she had done

the right thing. She'd been brave enough to save her people. The people were also glad Esther had risked her life to save them.

"Esther was brave, wasn't she?" Valerie said. "She did the right thing, even though she thought she might die."

"She was very brave," agreed Valerie's mother. "You are brave, too. You just have to find the strength to do what's right."

"I think I'll go upstairs and pray about this, Mom," Valerie told her mother. "I'm sure that God will help me find the strength I need."

"I'm sure he will, too, sweetheart," said her mother. "I think that praying

the other kids tried to pick on the new girl, I told them to stop. I asked them how they would feel if somebody treated them that way. They all said they were sorry and that they wouldn't do it anymore."

"That's great," said Valerie's mother.

"But wait, Mom, that's not all. I asked the new girl to be my study partner. She's coming over this afternoon."

is just the right thing to do."

The next afternoon Valerie was so excited, she ran all the way home from school. "Mom," she cried as she burst into the kitchen. "Guess what?"

"What, Valerie?" her mother said.

"I did the right thing!" Valerie said, proudly. "Today, when

Valerie's mother gave her a heartwarming smile. Just at that moment, the doorbell rang.

"That's her!" Valerie cried as she rushed to the door. "Mom," she said as she closed the door behind her visitor. "This is my new friend, Suzanne."

"I'm pleased to meet you, Suzanne," said Valerie's mother. "Welcome to our home."

Why Me?

"I need someone to be in charge of the science fair," said the teacher. She looked at each of the students in her classroom. "This is a very important job. This person must be a good organizer and understand responsibility. Ian, I choose you."

Ian sat up very straight in his seat when he heard his teacher choose him.

He sat up so straight he thought he could feel his hair stand up on his neck. Ian didn't like to admit it, but he was scared. *Me, in charge of the science fair?* he thought. *Why would she choose me to do that?*

He was still new to this school and sometimes he felt that he didn't fit in yet. He thought that might make his new job twice as hard.

"Are you sure you want me to choose a theme for the science fair, Mrs. Williams?" he asked when the school day was over and everyone else had gone home. "I still don't know very many people here. Maybe one of the other kids would do a better job."

"I'm sure you'll do a great job, Ian," Mrs. Williams told him. "That's the reason I chose you."

It made Ian feel good to know his teacher believed in him. But he still wasn't sure he could do such an important job.

"I know it must be scary to feel like you've been given a job that's too big for you, Ian," Mrs. Williams said. "But sometimes, when you know other people believe in you, you can surprise yourself. Just like Gideon did."

"Who?" Ian asked.

"Gideon," said Mrs. Williams. "He lived a long time ago."

Gideon and his people lived in the land that God had given them. But there was a problem. An enemy had moved in and was slowly stealing their food. Soon they would have no food at all.

Often Gideon wished his enemies would just go away. They were bigger and stronger and had better weapons. Gideon and his people didn't know what to do.

So, one day, God sent an angel to Gideon. The angel told Gideon that God had chosen him to lead his people against their enemies. With God's help, Gideon would win the battle without even fighting. He would give the people back their land and they would have food again.

When Gideon heard this, he was excited and frightened all at the same time. It was wonderful to think that his people might not have to worry about their enemies. But

Gideon didn't think he could accomplish such a big job.

So Gideon said to God, "Lord, if you have really chosen me to do this, give me a sign that what you say is true. I will set a piece of wool on the ground and leave it there overnight. In the morning, if there is dew on the piece of wool but not on the ground, then I will know that you have chosen me."

Then Gideon put the piece of wool on the ground and went to bed.

In the morning, he got up very early, and he hurried to the place where the piece of wool lay. Sure enough, just as he had requested, the ground around the piece of wool was dry, but the piece of wool was wet with morning dew. It was so wet that when Gideon picked the piece of wool up and squeezed it, a whole bowlful of water came out.

But Gideon still didn't think he was

the right one for the job. He wanted to make sure he was God's choice.

So Gideon said to God, "Please don't be angry with me. Let me ask just one more thing. Tonight when I set the piece of wool down, make the piece of wool dry and let the ground around it be wet. If you will do this, then I will know that you have chosen me to save my people."

And Gideon put the piece of wool on the ground and went to bed.

In the morning, when Gideon got up, he saw that, once again, God had granted his request. The ground around the piece of wool was soaked with water, but the piece of wool itself was completely dry. Not even one drop of water fell from it when Gideon

squeezed it with all his might.

And so, finally, Gideon believed that God had chosen him. Then God told Gideon to call an army together secretly.

Now Gideon called together an army. Thousands of men joined him to fight. But when all the men were together, God said to Gideon, "This is too big an army. Let anyone who trembles with fear go home."

So Gideon said, "Any man who trembles with fear at the thought of fighting our enemies can go home." Many men did this.

But still, God thought Gideon's army was too big. He said, "There are too many men. When they beat the enemy, they will think that they did it. You must send even more men home."

God said, "Take the men down to the water and have them take a drink. Separate those who lap the water with their tongues from those who kneel down to drink."

Once Gideon had done this, God chose the 300 men who had lapped the water. Then he told Gideon how to beat his enemies without fighting them. Gideon waited until it was night. Then he picked up a torch, an empty clay jar, and a trumpet. He told his soldiers to do the same. They put the torches inside the jars so the enemy wouldn't see them coming. Then they quietly crept to the edge of the enemy camp.

"Watch me," Gideon whispered to his soldiers. "Follow my lead and do exactly as I do."

Gideon took out his torch. He blew a loud note on his trumpet. And he pounded on his jar with all his might. Instantly, all of Gideon's soldiers did the same. They made a noise so loud, and a light so bright, that the men in the enemy camp were afraid for their lives. They were so scared that they began fighting each other. Then they ran away.

Gideon and his men had won without even having to fight, just as God had said they would.

"You really do believe in me, don't you?" Ian asked Mrs. Williams. "Even though I'm a little scared?"

"Yes, I do," Mrs. Williams answered. "Remember, Gideon was scared at first. But when he knew that God believed in him, he went out and beat his enemies without even fighting."

"I will do my best for you," Ian promised her. "I'm sure we'll have the best science fair ever."

"I knew I could count on you," Mrs. Williams said. "I'll see you tomorrow." Then she waved good-bye, got into her car, and drove away.

All the way home, Ian thought about the science fair. He thought about how Gideon had stopped being afraid when he knew that he was a part of God's plan.

By the time he got home, Ian was feeling much better. The phone rang the minute he stepped through the door. It was Wallace White,

the smartest kid in school. He wanted to help with the science fair, too.

Now Ian was proud that he had been chosen to come up with a theme for the science fair. It didn't seem so scary anymore. He knew that Mrs. Williams believed in him.

And Mrs. Williams was right about something else, Ian thought as he hung up the phone. It would be nice to make some new friends.

The Clean-up

"Hey, everybody! Ned's home!" Ned's younger brother, Matthew, yelled. And sure enough, when they got to the front door, Ned's whole family could see him coming up the front steps. Everybody was excited. This was the first time that Ned had come home since he'd joined the army.

"You look sharp in that uniform, son," Ned's father told him as he gave him a hug.

"Thanks, Dad," Ned answered. He saw that his dad was wearing the shirt he'd sent him for Father's Day. "You look pretty good yourself."

"Welcome home, Ned," said his mother. Ned gave her such a big hug he lifted her all the way off the ground.

"What about me? How do I look?" asked Matthew. Matthew was much younger than Ned, and he thought Ned was the greatest brother in the world.

"You look at least two inches taller, pipsqueak," Ned answered. "What's Mom been feeding you?" And everybody laughed and went into the house.

Ned and Matt's mother had made a wonderful dinner, and they ate until they couldn't eat another bite. Then Ned and Matthew did what they always did after dinner in the summertime. They went to sit on the front steps. They watched some of Matt's friends playing baseball in the street.

"Things look pretty much the same around here," Ned said. "It's almost as if I haven't been gone at all."

Suddenly, a car came racing around the corner, beeping its horn. All the baseball players raced to get out of the way. One of the boys said, "It's just too dangerous to play ball in the street." So they walked over to say

hello to Ned and Matt.

"Why are you guys playing baseball in the street?" Ned asked Matt's friends. "What's the matter with the old vacant lot? That's where we used to play."

Nobody answered for a moment. Everybody looked uncomfortable and sad. "We can't use the lot anymore," Matt finally told his brother. "Some people have started dumping stuff there. The lot is almost filled up with junk, and it's not a safe place to play."

"Did you ask them to stop?" Ned asked.

Matt and his friends nodded. "Yes, but the people got mad. They said we couldn't tell them what to do. They were big guys, Ned. It was scary. So we decided it was better to leave them alone."

Ned didn't say anything for a moment. He looked over at the vacant lot. "This reminds me of old General Nehemiah," he told Matt and his friends.

"General who?" Matt said. "What did he do? Is he one of your army buddies?"

"He was a general who lived a long time ago," Ned replied.

General Nehemiah worked for a very wealthy king. They were great friends. One day the king noticed that the general was very sad. "What is troubling you, Nehemiah?" the king asked him.

"I have just heard terrible news," Nehemiah answered,

"about Jerusalem, the town where I grew up. The walls have been torn down, and now the city is a junk pile. Once it was the most beautiful city in the world."

"I have heard stories of that city. What do you want to do?" asked the king.

"I have prayed to God to show me what to do. With your permission, I want to go back to Jerusalem and rebuild its walls," Nehemiah answered. "I hope that you will let me do this."

Now, King Artaxerxes remembered that the general had always done good work for him, so he agreed to let him go to Jerusalem and rebuild the walls. Nehemiah gave thanks to God. Then he set out upon his journey.

When the general got to Jerusalem, he rode around the city. He saw that all the walls had been destroyed by fire. There was junk everywhere. It would take a lot of time and effort to clean everything up and rebuild the walls. But the general knew that God would help him complete the great task. He knew that rebuilding the walls of Jerusalem was what God wanted him to do.

So he called together the people of Jerusalem and said, "We are in great trouble. The walls of Jerusalem have been torn down and other tribes are using our beautiful city as a dump. We can rebuild the walls together, if we all work hard." The people were glad that the general had come to help them.

But not everybody was happy that Nehemiah wanted to rebuild the walls. Around the city of Jerusalem there were many enemies. They did not want the city to be big and strong. They made fun of Nehemiah.

"You are not strong enough," they told him. "You will never be able to

rebuild the walls."

But Nehemiah didn't pay any attention to them. He knew that God would help him succeed. So Nehemiah gathered the people together and began rebuilding the walls.

Nehemiah and his friends worked hard, but the walls were very tall and there was a lot to do. When the walls were half as high as they needed to be, the enemies of Jerusalem said to Nehemiah:

"If you know what's good for you, you'll stop right now. If you don't stop working, we'll come back and fight with you. That will put a stop to rebuilding these walls!"

Some people were afraid. Some thought that maybe they should stop. But Nehemiah wasn't afraid. He asked all the workers to pray. Then the general got an idea. He divided his workers into families. Each family set up guards to watch for their enemies.

The enemies saw that Nehemiah and the families were ready for them. They also saw that God had given them courage and that they were not afraid. One evening, the enemies charged at one spot, but all the families came and

stood there. When the enemies saw this, they changed their minds and would not fight. Nehemiah and the families of Jerusalem continued rebuilding the walls.

Finally, the day came when the job was finished. The walls of Jerusalem once again rose tall and strong.

When their enemies saw what a good job Nehemiah and his friends had

done, it was their turn to be afraid.
They saw that God had helped
Nehemiah. So the enemies went away.
Nehemiah and all the families of
Jerusalem were happy.

Matt was quiet for a moment after
Ned had finished the story of General
Nehemiah. He was staring over at the
vacant lot.

"I'll bet we could clean up that
lot," he said, thoughtfully. "We'll
ask God to give us strength like he
gave Nehemiah."

"Cleaning up the lot would be a
good thing to do," Ned agreed. "And
I'm sure the neighbors would help you
if you asked them."

"It will be hard work," Matt said
to his friends, who were looking at
him seriously.

"I'll help you," one of Matt's
friends offered.

"Me too," another one said.

"I'll help, too," said Ned's father.
Everybody looked up.

"And so will I," said Ned's mom.

Ned's mom and dad had heard the whole story. "I'll call all the families in the neighborhood and ask them to help, too," said Ned's mom.

One by one, Matt's friends agreed to help him clean up the vacant lot. They liked the story of General Nehemiah, and they all wanted to work together to have a safe place to play.

"Maybe," Matt said, "maybe we should pray and ask God to help us. Dad, do you want to pray?"

"Normally I would, son. But I think that Ned should," answered his father.

Matthew bowed his head while Ned prayed. "I'm sure glad you're home, Ned," Matt said when the prayer was over.

"It's great to be home, little brother," Ned replied.

Then a neighbor called out, "I could use a little help over here."

Matt smiled as he said, "I'm ready. Let's go." And all of the families came together to help clean up their neighborhood.

The Really Big Storm

Kaboom! said the loud voice of the thunder. Alone in her bedroom, Echo pulled the covers over her head. Echo didn't like storms. They always scared her.

Echo could hear the sound of the wind outside her bedroom's large French doors. But at least the thunder was quiet for now. Gathering her courage, she pulled down the covers just enough to peek out with one eye. She wanted to see her rainbow nightlight. Echo had picked it out herself, and looking at it always made her feel better.

Just at that moment, a flash of lightning filled the room. It looked as if Echo had turned all her bedroom

lights on. But when the lightning was over, Echo could see that the nightlight had gone out. *Kaboom*, said the thunder. Then the big French doors flew open, and the wind and rain came into Echo's room. *Kaboom, boom BOOM!* Echo was too scared to stay by herself any longer. She was just about to scramble out of bed when her broth-er, Kit, appeared with a flashlight at the door to her room.

Kit and Echo were a good team as brother and sister. They almost always got along. And they *always* helped each other when one of them was in trouble. So Echo knew that Kit would help her now. Together they closed the French doors. Then Echo

followed Kit down the hall to his room.

"This storm scares me," said Echo as she huddled on the rug by Kit's bed. "I'll bet there's never been a bigger storm."

"You know what, Echo?" Kit said. "I know a story about the biggest storm that ever was. When you hear about *that* storm, I'll bet this one won't scare you at all."

"A bigger storm than this one?" Echo repeated. She could hardly believe that there had ever been a bigger storm.

"Yep," Kit answered. He took his flashlight and got a book out of his bookcase. Then he sat next to Echo on

the bed, and this is the story he read:

A long time ago, God looked down upon the earth, and what he saw made him both sad and angry. For he saw that the people he had made had forgotten all about him. They did bad things.

God looked all over the earth to try to find one good person. Finally, he saw Noah. Noah was a very good man who loved God. He worked very hard, and he enjoyed life with his family.

One day, God told Noah, "I am going to send a big flood to wash away all the evil in the world. Then the earth will be fresh and new again."

To get ready for the flood, God told Noah exactly what to do, and

Noah did everything just as God commanded him.

Noah built an ark of gopher wood. It was three stories tall and had lots of rooms in it. He put a great door in the side and painted it with pitch so it wouldn't leak.

When the ark was finished, God sent Noah two of every kind of animal that lived upon the earth. There were animals that walked along the ground like hippos, lions, zebras, and bears. And there were birds and butterflies that flew through the air. Noah scratched his chin and smiled in amusement as they began to arrive.

Then God said to Noah, "In seven

days, I will send rain." It was time for Noah to load his family and the animals onto the ark.

God told Noah that he was going

to send a great rainstorm upon the earth. For forty days and forty nights, there would be thunder and lightning the likes of which the world had never seen.

When Noah and his family heard this, they trembled. But then Noah said to them, "Do not be afraid. We have obeyed God, and so, when the great storm comes, he won't forget us. We will be safe inside the ark while the storm is raging. When it is all over, we can come out again."

Noah's family was comforted by his words, and they went into the ark when God told them to. Then God closed the ark's great door and, as soon as he had done this, the first drops of rain began to fall.

The storm that God sent upon the earth was greater than anything Noah and his family could have imagined. Never in their lives had they seen such a storm. The water rose so high that it covered the top of every mountain.

But no matter how hard it rained, no matter how bright the lightning or loud the thunder, Noah and his family knew that they and all the animals were safe inside the ark.

Finally, there came a day when the storm was over. No more rain fell from the sky. There was no more lightning and no more thunder. The earth was filled with a great wind. The wind made the water go lower and lower. Soon, the tops of the mountains reappeared.

One day, Noah decided it was time to open a window. Noah let a dove fly out and waited to see what would happen.

Noah waited a long time for the dove and all of his family wondered what was happening. But, finally,

the dove came back because it couldn't find a place to land. So, Noah knew the water wasn't low enough. It was not yet time to leave the ark.

Noah waited seven days and then he let the dove fly out again. This time, when the dove came back, it had a leaf from an olive tree in its mouth. So Noah knew that the water was below the treetops. But that still wasn't low enough. It was not yet

time to leave the ark.

Noah sent the dove out once again. This time, the dove didn't come back. At last! The dove had found a dry place to land. Now Noah knew that the water was low enough. Finally, it was time to leave the ark. Noah opened the great door, and all of his family and all of the animals came out. It was good to be in the warm sunshine. It was good to stand on dry land again. The whole earth was fresh and new.

Noah and his family gave thanks to God for keeping them safe. And there, in the sky above them, were great arches of shining color. Noah and his family had never seen such a thing before.

"This is a rainbow, Noah," the Lord told them. "And it is a sign of the promise I make to you now. I promise that never again will I make a storm such as this one. Never again will water completely

cover up the earth. From now on, all people can take comfort from this when they see my rainbow in the sky."

Noah thought the rainbow was beautiful, and he was happy that he and his family were alive. Now Noah, his family, and all the animals were free to roam the earth.

"God can protect me from this storm, can't he, Kit?" Echo asked her brother when the story was over. "He can protect me when I am afraid."

"Yes, he can, Echo," Kit answered. "But always remember, first we have to ask."

"I'll remember," Echo promised. "Thank you for reading me the story of Noah's ark. And you were right about this storm. Noah's storm was much worse than this one! I think I'll go back to bed now."

"Do you want me to go with you?" Kit asked.

"No, thank you," said Echo. "I am not afraid."

Echo walked

to her room by herself and climbed back under her covers. Just as she did, the power came back on. Echo could see her rainbow night-light glowing near the doorway. Now it made her feel better than ever before.

Every time she looked at her rainbow, Echo knew she'd remember that first rainbow that God had put up in the sky. And she'd remember that God would always protect her, if she asked him to. This made Echo very, very happy.

"Thank you, God," she whispered as she fell fast asleep. And the loud voice of the thunder never frightened her again.